Making Faces!

Nancy and Bess met outside school. They couldn't wait to see all the election posters in their classroom.

As the girls walked down the hallway, Nancy could hear some of the kids from their classroom talking.

When Nancy and Bess walked into the room, it got silent. Then they saw it.

The poster that Bess had made was hanging on the wall. The picture still looked like Jessie, but someone had taken off the rainbow and the butterfly that Bess had traced and colored so carefully.

Now something else was on the poster. A thin, squiggly black mustache.

The Nancy Drew Notebooks

Available from MINSTREL Books

#14

THE NANCY DREW NOTEBOOKS®

THE FUNNY FACE FIGHT

CAROLYN KEENE

Illustrated by Anthony Accardo

A MINSTREL® BOOK

PUBLISHED BY POCKET BOOKS

New York   London   Toronto   Sydney   Tokyo   Singapore

This book is a work of fiction. Names, characters, places and incidents are products of the author's imagination or are used fictitiously. Any resemblance to actual events or locales or persons, living or dead, is entirely coincidental.

A MINSTREL PAPERBACK *Original*

 A Minstrel Book published by
POCKET BOOKS, a division of Simon & Schuster Inc.
1230 Avenue of the Americas, New York, NY 10020

Copyright © 1996 by Simon & Schuster Inc.
Produced by Mega-Books of New York, Inc.

ISBN: 0-671-53553-6

First Minstrel Books printing September 1996

10 9 8 7 6 5 4 3 2 1

NANCY DREW, THE NANCY DREW NOTEBOOKS, A MINSTREL BOOK and colophon are registered trademarks of Simon & Schuster Inc.

Cover art by Aleta Jenks

Printed in the U.S.A.

1

The Race Is On

Don't vote for Nancy Drew," Jason Hutchings chanted during recess. "She smells like a dirty old shoe."

Jason and his best friend, Mike Minelli, cracked up laughing.

It was Monday. Mrs. Reynolds's third-grade class was getting ready to hold an election for class president. After recess they would nominate candidates. Then they would vote on Friday.

"Well, I think Nancy would make a *great* president," Molly Angelo said.

"So do I," Jenny March added.

"No way!" Mike pinched his nose with his fingers. The two boys ran away yelling, "Peeuw, Nancy Drew! Peeuw, Nancy Drew!"

"You creeps!" Nancy shouted to them.

Molly shook her head. "They're mean."

Eight-year-old Nancy Drew pushed her long reddish blond hair behind her shoulder and nodded.

"It's okay, Molly," Nancy said. "I don't want to be president anyway. Bess and George already asked me."

"Oh, come on, Nancy," Jenny said. *"I'll* nominate you. It will be neat to have a detective for class president."

"But the president has lots to do. Like helping with Fall Festival and class trips," Nancy said. "I already take ballet lessons and play soccer. I wouldn't have time to be president."

"Hey, Nancy, guess what?" Bess Marvin called from across the school yard. Bess was one of Nancy's best friends. Nancy went to join her.

"I'm going to nominate Jessie Shapiro for president. You'll help get her elected, won't you?"

Before Nancy could answer, George Fayne came over to them. George's real name was Georgia. Nobody called her that, though. She was Nancy's other best friend.

George and Bess were cousins. But they rarely agreed on anything. They didn't look alike either. Bess had long blond hair, and George had short, curly dark hair.

"I just asked Vicki Wolf if she wanted to be class president," George said. "And she said yes. Isn't that great?"

"What's so great about that?" Bess asked. "Vicki just joined the soccer team. She's on the town softball team, too. Isn't that enough?"

"That's the point," George told her. "Vicki's a great athlete. If she gets elected, she'll do a lot for sports, especially for the soccer team."

George and Nancy both played on the third-grade soccer team—the Tigers. Bess didn't.

"Well, if Jessie's elected," Bess said, "she'll do things for *everybody,* not just

3

for soccer players. And you should have talked to us before you asked Vicki to run. We're your friends, aren't we?"

George looked surprised. "Of course, Bess. You guys are my best friends. But I still want Vicki to be president."

George turned to Nancy. "I'm going to ask all the Tigers in our class to vote for Vicki. How about it, Nancy?"

Bess put her hand on Nancy's arm. "You'll vote for Jessie, won't you? Remember, I asked you first."

Nancy didn't know what to do. She liked both Vicki and Jessie. And George and Bess were both her best friends. Whatever she did, somebody's feelings might be hurt.

"Jessie has some super ideas," Bess added. "Like a class trip to Water World. Her dad knows the man who runs it."

"That sounds like fun," Nancy said. "And Bess *did* ask me first. I guess I'll be on Jessie's side."

"Well, if that's the way you feel," George said. She turned and walked away.

Bess watched her go. "I hope George isn't mad," she said.

"She'll be okay," Nancy told her.

Just then a soccer ball came bouncing across the pavement. It hit Bess in the arm.

"Ow!" Bess shouted. "That hurt!"

Nancy looked around. Vicki was standing nearby with her best friend, Lizzie Artello. George was with them now. All three of them were giggling.

"Sorry, Bess," Vicki called out.

Bess tossed the ball to them. "I can't believe they hit me," she said to Nancy. "That was really mean. And George thought it was funny."

Bess was right, Nancy thought. If they hit Bess on purpose, that *was* mean.

After recess all the kids returned to the classroom and took their seats. Mrs. Reynolds stood in the front of the room.

Mrs. Reynolds used to be called Ms. Spencer. When she got married, she changed her name to Mrs. Reynolds.

"It's time for nominations," Mrs. Reynolds said. "If there's someone you think should be class president, raise your hand and tell us who it is. Then someone else needs to second the nomination. May I see hands?"

Bess, George, Lizzie, and Jason all raised their hands. Mrs. Reynolds called on Lizzie first.

"I nominate Vicki Wolf," Lizzie said loudly.

"Does anyone second that nomination?" Mrs. Reynolds asked.

George turned and glanced at Bess. Then George raised her hand. "I second it."

Next, Bess nominated Jessie. Nancy raised her hand and said, "Me, too."

Then Jason spoke in a deep voice like a television announcer. "The one, the only, Mike Minelli!"

Everyone laughed. They all knew that Jason and Mike were best friends.

Peter DeSands jumped up. "I second Mike," he said loudly. "Not only that, I third and fourth him, too!"

"Thank you, Peter." Mrs. Reynolds grinned. "Our three candidates are Jessie, Vicki, and Mike."

Everybody clapped.

"Now we're going to spend some time working on the stories you've been writing," Mrs. Reynolds continued. "The three candidates may work on their campaign speeches. We'll all get to hear the speeches on Thursday."

Nancy opened her English notebook. She had already finished a story about three friends who lived on the beach. Now she decided to write a story about her puppy, Chocolate Chip. Chip was a chocolate-colored Labrador retriever. At the top of the page Nancy wrote, "Chip and the Missing Bone." Then she drew two lines under the words.

What next? Nancy tried to think. It was always hard to start a story. She sat back and looked around the room.

Mike was chewing on his pen, and Jenny was staring at the chalkboard. Two rows ahead, Vicki was writing on index cards. She put them in a stack near the edge of her desk.

Bess got up from her seat and walked toward the dictionary stand next to Mrs. Reynolds's desk. As she passed

Vicki's desk, she bumped against it. Vicki's stack of cards tumbled off the desktop and scattered across the floor.

"My speech!" Vicki screamed.

"You did that on purpose, Bess Marvin," an angry voice said.

Nancy looked over her shoulder. Lizzie and Brenda Carlton had gotten up from their desks. They were standing behind Nancy. Brenda was writing in her red reporter's notebook.

Brenda wrote her own newspaper. It was called the *Carlton News*. She printed it on her father's computer. What Brenda liked most were stories that made other kids look bad.

George jumped up from her seat to look at the mess next to Vicki's desk.

Bess looked at George. But George didn't say anything.

"It was an accident," Bess said. Her voice almost cracked. "I didn't do it on purpose."

"You did, too," Lizzie said. Then she turned to Brenda. "Bess is trying to make Vicki lose," she said. "I know it!"

2

Dirty Tricks

ess," Mrs. Reynolds said, "please help Vicki pick up her cards. The rest of you, return to your seats."

George sat down, and Lizzie went back to her desk. Brenda walked over to Vicki's desk instead.

"So, you think some people are playing dirty tricks to win the class election," Brenda said to Vicki. She looked directly at Bess. "Is that right?"

Vicki glanced at Bess, too. Then she lowered her eyes. "I guess so," she said.

Mrs. Reynolds stood up from her desk. "Brenda, I said go back to your seat."

Brenda gave Nancy a smug look. "Don't worry, Vicki," she said as she walked back to her desk. "They won't get away with it. Just wait until you read my special Election Day issue."

Bess leaned close to Nancy as she slid back into her own seat. "What is she talking about?" she asked.

Nancy shrugged. "You never know with Brenda."

Nancy tried to concentrate on her story about Chip again. But something was bothering her, and it wasn't Brenda. Lizzie said Bess had knocked down Vicki's speech on purpose. George hadn't even stuck up for Bess. Maybe George *was* mad at Bess for choosing Jessie, Nancy thought. Maybe George was mad at Nancy, too.

On Tuesday Mrs. Reynolds passed out some small paper plates with safety pins taped to the back.

"You can draw or paint on your plate to make a campaign button," she explained to the class. "Then on Election Day, you can wear the button to show which candidate you prefer."

"But I'm not sure who I want to vote for," Jenny said.

Mrs. Reynolds smiled. "If you're undecided, you can start decorating your button now. Later you can fill in the name of the candidate."

Nancy had a great idea for a button. She went to a table at the back of the room to paint her plate. So did Bess.

George and Vicki were at another table a few feet away. Bess looked at them.

"I just know George is mad at me because I want Jessie to win," she whispered to Nancy.

"I think she might be mad at both of us," Nancy said. "Let's ask her to come over to my house after school."

Jason Hutchings came up to their table. He had a long paintbrush in one hand and a jar of red paint in the other.

"You're both making buttons for Mike, right?" He looked over Nancy's shoulder.

"Mike who?" Nancy said.

"Yeah." Bess grinned, going along

with Nancy's teasing. "I don't know *anybody* named Mike."

"Ha-ha," Jason said. "That was so funny I forgot to laugh."

"But you just did." Nancy giggled. Bess laughed, too.

"Well, Mike's going to make the cafeteria stop serving macaroni and cheese," Jason said. "It's gross."

Some of the kids nearby cheered. Everybody hated the macaroni and cheese.

"I'm for Jessie," Bess told him. "She'll get us a trip to Water World."

"And Vicki will help the soccer team," George called from the other table. "I'm voting for her."

Jason walked over to George and Vicki. "That's a great button, George," he said.

Nancy looked over. George had drawn a smiley face on her plate. Around the edge it said, Be Happy— Vote Vicki.

"But it needs something," Jason went on. "I know. A beard and glasses!" He acted as if he was about to paint on George's button.

"No way!" George held up her paint-brush like a sword. "On guard!"

Jason and George pretended to have a sword fight with their brushes.

"George, Jason, stop that at once," Mrs. Reynolds called.

"This isn't the end of it," Jason said. Then he walked to his desk.

Laughing, George turned to Vicki. She put her arm around her.

"Lucky him," she said. "I was just about to paint a *V* for Vicki on his shirt!"

After school Nancy and Bess waited by the front entrance for George to come out. George walked out with Vicki. Lizzie was a few steps behind them.

"George?" Bess called. "You want to do something this afternoon?"

"Sorry. I'm doing something with Vicki and Lizzie today," George said. "See you tomorrow." She walked off with Vicki and Lizzie.

Bess looked sad. "It looks like George found two new best friends," she said.

"George wouldn't do that," Nancy said. She wanted to cheer Bess up. "I know—let's take Chip to the park."

Bess was still looking at George, Vicki, and Lizzie. "That sounds like fun," she said, but she didn't sound happy.

"Chip has been expecting you," Hannah Gruen said to Nancy. "At three o'clock she starts watching the back door."

Hanna was the Drew family's housekeeper. She had lived with Nancy and her father ever since Nancy's mother died.

"Good girl!" Nancy said. She bent down to rub her puppy's ears. Right away Chip covered Nancy's face with sloppy wet kisses.

Nancy and Bess quickly ate a snack of cookies and cider. Nancy grabbed her soccer ball from the hall closet. Bess snapped Chip's leash to her collar. Then they were off to the park.

At the park, Nancy took off Chip's leash. Bess tossed the soccer ball and Chip ran after it. The puppy tried to catch the ball in her mouth. It was too big. She jumped on it with her front paws. Then she bumped it with her head.

"Look," Nancy said. "Chip's learning to play soccer!"

Nancy and Bess ran over to the puppy. Nancy gave the ball a light kick. Chip chased it and bumped it with her nose.

"You were right, Nancy. This is fun!" Bess kicked the ball back to the puppy.

Chip yipped loudly and stopped it with her paws.

"Great block, Chip," Nancy called. "Now kick it. Go for the goal!"

Instead, Chip turned and bolted across the park. Nancy and Bess ran after her. Chip stopped to sniff around a picnic table. Then she jumped onto the table.

"Chip, get down!" Nancy shouted. As she got closer, she saw that George, Vicki, and Lizzie were sitting at the table. They had been working on a poster. Now Chip was dancing around on top of it, smearing the paint with her paws and nose.

George was laughing. Lizzie wasn't.

"Nancy Drew!" Lizzie said. "Can't you make your dog behave? I bet you told her to come over and ruin our work!"

"She just wants to play," George said. She reached over to pet the puppy. "It's okay, Lizzie. I'll make another poster."

"I'm really sorry, guys." Nancy put the leash back on Chip.

Lizzie grabbed their paints and poster and hurried away. Vicki and George went after her.

Bess and Nancy watched as George and Vicki caught up to Lizzie. George gave Lizzie a friendly punch on the arm. It looked like George was trying to make her feel better.

"I can't believe George didn't even say hi to us," Bess said. "And why is Lizzie being so mean?"

"I don't know, Bess." Nancy watched

the three girls walk out of the park. She was wondering the same thing herself.

Nancy bent down and gave Chip a hug. She had hoped Bess was wrong about George finding two new best friends. But now it looked as though Bess might be right.

3

Beard on a Button

That's not funny!" Nancy heard George say in an angry voice. Nancy and Bess had just entered the classroom on Wednesday morning. There was a big crowd at the back of the room. Nancy and Bess hurried to see what was going on.

"Who did this?" George demanded.

Nancy stood on her tiptoes and looked past the crowd. George was holding up her Be Happy—Vote Vicki button. Taped over the smiley face was another face—a funny face with glasses and a big black beard.

"See, George, I was right," Jason said. "Your button looks a lot better now."

20

A bunch of kids were laughing. But George didn't think it was funny.

"I'll pay you back for this, Jason," she said. George sounded really angry. Almost as angry as when someone called her Georgia.

"I didn't do it, George," Jason said. "But it does look funny."

"Hey, Vicki," Mike said. "Are you going to grow a beard now?"

Everyone kept laughing. Then Lizzie grabbed the button from George.

"Somebody's trying to ruin Vicki's campaign," she said. "And I know who." She put her hands on her hips and looked right at Bess.

"George is my cousin and my best friend," Bess said. "I would never do anything like that to her. Right, George?"

George didn't answer. She was busy trying to remove the funny face from her button. She didn't want to tear the paper.

Then Lizzie turned to Brenda. Brenda was writing in her reporter's notebook. She was standing right next to Lizzie.

"Brenda, I want to talk to you about Bess and her dirty tricks," Lizzie said. "Meet me after school."

Bess was still staring at George. She waited a moment. Then she whirled around and stomped away.

Nancy started to go after Bess. But just then George got the funny face off. Her button was okay.

"Can I have the drawing, George?" Nancy asked. George gave it to her.

Nancy looked at the drawing. It was done on tracing paper. It had a lot of sticky tape on the back. George was lucky she didn't ruin her button when she peeled the drawing off, Nancy thought.

"Are you going to find out who did this?" George asked.

"Maybe," Nancy answered. "But I have to ask you a question first." Nancy took a deep breath. "Are you mad at Bess and me?"

"Well," George said. She looked at her feet. Then she looked at Nancy. "I

was mad at you for choosing Jessie. But not anymore. That wasn't fair."

George looked away from Nancy. "But I'm still mad at Bess," she said. "I know you're not going to believe this, but I think Bess—"

"Nancy? George? Will you take your seats please?" Mrs. Reynolds said from the front of the room.

George didn't have time to finish her sentence. She went to her desk.

What was George going to say? Nancy wondered. Did she really think that Bess was pulling mean tricks on Vicki?

Nancy walked back to her seat. She looked at the funny face. Yesterday Jason had said George's button needed a beard and glasses. He even said that their paint fight wasn't over. Could this be what he meant?

Nancy decided that Jason was her first suspect in this mystery. Now she needed proof. Whoever made the face had to have tracing paper, she thought. This was a big clue.

As Nancy passed Jason's desk, she

looked over his shoulder. He had just taken everything out of his backpack. Nancy saw a notebook, a library book, and a pad of yellow paper—but no tracing paper. Maybe he had it at home, Nancy thought.

Nancy sat down at her desk. She took out her special notebook. It had a shiny blue cover and a pocket on the inside. Nancy's father had given it to her to help her solve mysteries.

Nancy put the funny face drawing in the pocket. Then she turned to a new page and wrote, "The Funny Face Mystery." She drew two lines under the words. Under them she wrote:

Suspects
Jason

Nancy thought and thought. Then she remembered Brenda talking about an Election Day story for her paper. Could Brenda have done the funny face for her story? She was always doing mean things. Nancy wrote down Brenda's name.

Nancy couldn't think of anyone else. Two suspects and no proof. This was going to be a tough case.

Later, in the lunchroom, Nancy saw George sitting next to Vicki. They were eating and laughing. Lizzie sat across from them.

Bess and Jessie were at a different table. Bess looked upset. Nancy took her tray and sat down next to her.

"Why is Lizzie saying all these mean things about me?" Bess asked. "I wouldn't be mean to Vicki, and I wouldn't do anything to George's button."

"I know," Nancy said. "It doesn't make any sense."

"And why is George sitting over there?" Bess continued. "What did we ever do to her?" A few tears rolled down Bess's cheeks.

"Don't cry, Bess," Jessie said.

Nancy didn't say anything. She didn't want to tell Bess the truth—that George really *was* mad at Bess, that

George thought Bess had taped the funny face onto her button.

"Well, if George is mad at us, then I'm mad at her, too." Bess wiped her tears away with the back of her hand. "She's not my cousin anymore either. I never want to see her again!"

Nancy felt awful. What if her two best friends never talked to each other again? She had to solve this case fast.

After lunch it was time for math. Nancy loved to do math problems. She thought they were just like solving puzzles, kind of like mysteries.

Nancy glanced over at Bess. Bess was taking everything out of her desk. She was looking for her math book. Then Nancy saw something that made her heart sink. Underneath Bess's language arts book was a pad of tracing paper.

Nancy couldn't believe it. Bess was now her number one suspect.

4

A Poster Prank

I'm going to make a great election poster," Bess said to Nancy.

Mrs. Reynolds was giving the class time to finish their buttons. The kids who were finished with their buttons were allowed to make posters.

Mrs. Reynolds would hang up the posters after school. On Thursday Jessie, Vicki, and Mike would give their speeches.

Nancy worked on her button. She saw Bess take out a pair of scissors, some glue, markers, a magazine, and the pad of tracing paper Nancy had seen earlier.

"I'm going to use this picture," Bess

said, cutting it out of the magazine. "It sort of looks like Jessie," Bess said.

Nancy looked at the picture. "Wow, it does," she agreed. But Nancy couldn't stop thinking of the tracing paper. She had to know why Bess had it.

"Um, what's the tracing paper for?" Nancy asked. She tried to sound as if nothing was wrong.

Bess picked up the pad. "To trace a picture of a rainbow and a butterfly. I'm going to color them and paste them on the girl's face. It's supposed to look like face painting. That's one of Jessie's ideas for the Fall Festival."

Nancy looked at the tracing paper. It looked just like the paper used for the funny face. But Nancy wasn't sure. She needed to get a closer look.

"Could I have a sheet of it, too?" she asked Bess.

"Sure," Bess said. She ripped out a piece and gave it to Nancy.

Nancy took the paper. When Bess wasn't looking, she tucked it into her blue notebook. She would look at it later.

Bess finished her poster. Nancy finished her button. She had drawn some squares and written:

```
          C
          L   P
      B   A   R
    J E S S I E
      S   S   S
      T
```

The letters were painted in bright colors.

"Oh, excellent!" Bess said when she saw Nancy's button. "It's a crossword!"

Jessie came over to look, too. "That is so cool," she said.

Jason came over and looked at Bess's poster. He was wearing his button. "Hey, how about painting a bird on her nose?" he said. "A buzzard!"

"I think Bess's poster is very artistic," Jessie said. "Not like what you did." She stared at Jason's button. It just said "Mike" in big red letters.

Jason grinned. "At least people know what my button means."

Nancy looked at Bess and Jessie and rolled her eyes. "What does he know?"

The last bell rang. It was time to go home. All the kids went to their cubbies—except for Phoebe Archer and Nancy. Today Mrs. Reynolds said Phoebe could wash the chalkboard. Nancy wanted to look at Bess's tracing paper.

She took it out from the pocket of her blue notebook. Then she took out the piece of paper with the funny face on it.

Nancy studied them both. Bess's paper was a little lighter. It felt smoother, too. Nancy held it up to the light. She could see the faint words *Heron Papers*. She knew that was called a watermark.

On the other paper, Nancy saw the faint letters *He* and part of the letter *w*. The watermark must have been cut off, Nancy thought. But that didn't matter. There was no *w* in *Heron*.

Nancy felt like cheering. The two papers were not the same. Bess was innocent after all!

Now Nancy had to get Bess and George to make up. She ran out to the cubbies.

"Do you guys want to come over to my house?" Nancy asked them.

"Sure," Bess said.

"I can't," George said at the same time. "Vicki and I are doing something."

Bess frowned. She squinted her eyes and looked at George. "Another election meeting?" she asked.

George looked away. "Uh, no," George said. "We're just going to kick a soccer ball around. See you tomorrow."

Bess was silent on the walk to Nancy's house. Nancy was disappointed. She had wanted to tell George her news.

Bess and Nancy were just going inside Nancy's house when George came running up.

"Nancy, Bess," George called. "Can I still come over?"

"Sure," Nancy said. "But what about Vicki?"

"Lizzie came over and asked Vicki to the mall. She said there wasn't room for me in her mom's car."

"That's too bad," Nancy said.

"That's okay," George said. "I didn't want to go with them anyway. Vicki's nice, but Lizzie said some really mean things about Bess." Then she looked at Bess. "I told Lizzie she was wrong."

"You did?" Bess said quietly.

George nodded. "Of course I did, Bess." George put one arm around Bess. She put the other arm around Nancy. "You and Nancy are my best friends. But, um, Bess?" George said. She stared down at her shoes. "You're not still mad at me. Are you?"

"No," Bess said. "I was only mad at you because you were mad at me."

George giggled.

"What's so funny?" Bess asked.

"I was only mad at *you*," George said, "because I thought *you* were mad at *me!*"

The three girls laughed. George, Bess, and Nancy squeezed into a huge hug.

No one was happier than Nancy. She had made a mistake. George didn't think Bess had taped the funny face to her button after all. Now they were all friends again.

"Let's go inside," Nancy said as she opened the front door and led her friends into the house. Chocolate Chip greeted them with her leash in her mouth.

Nancy smiled. "I think she's trying to tell us something."

Bess and George called their moms to tell them where they were. Then the girls took Chip out for her walk. They were heading for the park when they saw Jason coming down the street. He was holding a paper bag.

Jason waved and walked over. Then he bent down to pet Chip. The paper bag he was holding slipped out of his hand. A new package of black construction paper spilled onto the sidewalk.

"Oops," Jason said. He gave Chip one

last scratch under her chin. Then he picked up the paper and put it back in the bag. "So, have you decided to vote for Mike yet?" he asked the girls.

"Vote for Mike?" Bess scrunched up her face. "Not in a zillion years!"

The next morning Nancy, Bess, and George met outside school. They couldn't wait to see all the election posters in their classroom. The day before, Mrs. Reynolds had promised to hang them up after school.

As the girls walked down the hallway, Nancy could hear some of the kids from their classroom talking.

When Nancy, Bess, and George walked into the room, it got silent. Then they saw it.

The poster that Bess had worked so hard on the day before was hanging on the wall. The picture still looked like Jessie. But someone had taken off the rainbow and the butterfly that Bess had traced and colored so carefully.

Now something else was on the poster. A thin, squiggly black mustache.

5

Who Was Where?

Which one of you ruined my poster?"
Bess asked loudly. She walked right
over to Vicki and Lizzie. Vicki was sitting at her desk. Lizzie was leaning
over Vicki's desk, talking to her.

"Bess," Vicki said. "I didn't—"

"She's crazy!" Lizzie interrupted.
"Bess probably did it herself."

Nancy and George went over to
them. Some other kids gathered around
Vicki's desk, too.

"Why would she do a thing like
that?" Nancy said.

"To make people feel sorry for Jessie," Lizzie said. "So they would vote
for her."

"That's dumb," Nancy told her. She

looked around at the other kids. "Anyway, I *know* Bess didn't do it."

"How, Nancy?" Molly asked.

"Because yesterday we left school together. The poster was all right then. We were together all afternoon."

"Maybe she did it this morning," Jenny said.

Nancy shook her head. "We got to school at the same time. And that stupid mustache was already there."

"It's not such a bad mustache," Jason said thoughtfully. "It's very artistic."

Bess's face got red. "Jason, you—" she started to say.

Mrs. Reynolds came over. "What's the matter here?" she asked.

Several kids laughed and pointed at the mustache on Bess's poster.

Mrs. Reynolds frowned. "I don't think that's funny," she said. "In our classroom, we respect one another's work. Please go to your seats."

"May I take down my poster first?" Bess asked. "I want to fix it and put a new rainbow and butterfly on it."

"Of course you can, Bess," Mrs. Reynolds said.

"I'll help you," Nancy said.

Nancy and Bess stepped closer to the poster. They looked at the mustache. It was made out of black construction paper.

Bess grabbed Nancy's arm. "Nancy," she whispered, "remember Jason bought black construction paper yesterday?"

Nancy nodded as she took down Bess's poster. "Let's watch him."

Nancy and Bess took their seats.

It was time for the three candidates to make their speeches. Mrs. Reynolds wrote their names on slips of paper. She shook them in a bag, then pulled one out.

Jessie Shapiro was first. She stood up and walked to the front of the room. Nancy thought she looked a little nervous.

"I think we ought to go on lots of class trips—like to Water World," she said. "And for Fall Festival we should do really cool face painting. We could have fun and make money for charity, too. That's all."

Lots of kids clapped. Bess nudged Nancy. "All right!" she whispered.

Vicki was next. She had her stack of index cards in her hand. "I want team sports during recess. Right now all we do is run around," she said. "And on field trips, we could go watch the Tigers play soccer. Everybody cheering for us would help us win more games."

Vicki glanced down at her cards. Some of them slipped out of her hand. Vicki's face turned red. She bent down and picked them up.

"Oh, yeah," she said, straightening up. "Fall Festival. I'd like a booth where people toss balls at targets. That's fun."

Vicki sat down. People clapped for her, too.

It was Mike's turn. He ran to the front of the room chanting, "Down with macaroni! Down with macaroni!" When he reached the chalkboard, he stuck both hands up in the air and added, "And cheese!"

Everybody laughed. When they quieted down, he said, "I want to change our class pet to a frog. Or maybe a snake. A big one. We could take turns feeding it mice."

"Yuck!" someone shouted. "Gross!"

Mike's grin widened. "And for Fall Festival we could sell lemonade—with lots of hot sauce in it. People would have to pay extra for water. We'd make a fortune."

Jason jumped up and called out, "Boo! Sit down!"

Mike looked confused. "But, Jason, you're on my side," he said.

Jason grinned. "Sure I am. But if you keep talking, *nobody* will vote for you!"

Mike sat down. Everybody cheered.

After the speeches, the class headed outside for gym class. On the way, Nancy thought about the case. She was pretty sure Jason had done the funny faces. But she knew that anyone could have construction paper. There was even some in the art room. What she needed was a witness.

Nancy saw Phoebe Archer walking ahead of her. Maybe she saw someone, Nancy thought.

"Phoebe," Nancy called. She ran to catch up to her. "You stayed after school yesterday to clean the chalkboard, right?"

"Uh-huh," Phoebe said.

"Did anyone else come back into the room?" Nancy asked.

Phoebe thought for a minute. "Um— only Brenda. She came in when Mrs. Reynolds and I were leaving. She said she forgot something. Why?"

"Oh, nothing," Nancy said. "Did you notice Bess's poster?"

"Yes, Mrs. Reynolds hung it up," Phoebe said. "And it *didn't* have a mustache when I left."

Hmmm, Nancy thought. Brenda was in the classroom alone. Maybe Jason *didn't* do it. Brenda could have done it, too.

The gym teacher chose Molly and Peter to be team captains for kickball. Molly picked Jessie to be on her team.

Peter picked Mike. Then Molly chose Nancy.

Nancy walked over to where Jessie was standing while Molly and Peter finished choosing their teams.

"I hope you solve the mystery soon, Nancy," Jessie said. "Some of the kids are saying they won't vote for me. They think Bess ruined her own poster to help me win."

"Maybe you can help me," Nancy told her. "Was that mustache on Bess's poster when you got to class this morning?"

Jessie nodded. "I left it there because I wanted you to see it—for evidence."

"That was smart, Jessie," Nancy said. "Was anyone else in the room?"

"Jason, Lizzie, and Peter were there before me. Does that help?"

Nancy smiled. "I think so."

Only three kids had been in the classroom before Jessie. And one of them was one of her suspects—Jason. Nancy wanted to talk to him. And she was in luck. Molly had chosen Jason for their team.

Jason was with three other boys. They were practicing kicking a ball as hard as they could. Nancy waited until they stopped. Then she went over to Jason.

"That mustache on Bess's poster was made with black construction paper," Nancy said.

"I know," Jason said. "So?"

"So you bought some paper like that yesterday," Nancy said.

"Uh-huh," Jason said. "So?"

"So, did you make that mustache?" Nancy asked.

"Tell you what," Jason said with a teasing grin. "I'll give you a clue."

Jason reached into his pocket. When he pulled his hand out, he was holding a big black marker.

"See this?" he said. "When I make a mustache, it *stays* there!"

Jason took the cap off of his marker. He held the marker close to Nancy's face.

"Let me show you, Nancy," he said.

"Don't you dare, Jason," Nancy shouted. She backed away from him. Sometimes Jason Hutchings was really weird, Nancy thought. And she couldn't decide if he was telling the truth.

The kids played a long game of kick-ball. Molly's team won. When gym was over, Nancy's third-grade class returned to their room.

Everyone stopped by their cubbies to put away their coats. Nancy hung up her jacket and waved to Bess. Bess took out her notebook and turned to go into the classroom.

Then Nancy saw Lizzie grab Bess's arm.

"Bess!" Lizzie said loudly. "You stole my new notebook!"

6

Brenda Spreads the News

Let go of my arm!" Bess shouted at Lizzie.

"That's my new purple notebook," Lizzie insisted. "Give it back!"

"This is *my* purple notebook," Bess said. "I just took it out of my cubby."

Nancy ran over to where Bess and Lizzie were fighting. George did, too.

"Bess, I think you left your notebook on your desk," Nancy said.

Bess looked at Nancy. Then she opened the notebook. Lizzie's name was on the inside cover.

"Oops! Sorry." Bess handed Lizzie the notebook. "But I *did* get it from my cubby."

George stepped forward. "That's my fault, Bess," she said. "I saw the notebook on the floor. I thought it was yours, and I put it in my cubby. But then I was afraid I'd forget to give it to you. So I put it in your cubby instead."

"Okay, everyone," Mrs. Reynolds said, "let's go inside the classroom."

At noon everybody lined up in the hall to go to the cafeteria. Mr. Putnam was walking toward the class. Nancy knew he worked in the principal's office. He was carrying a big brown envelope.

"Somebody dropped this off for Brenda Carlton," Mr. Putnam said to Mrs. Reynolds.

Brenda walked over and took the envelope.

"It's the *Carlton News*," she announced. "Special election issue. Get your copy here!"

Everybody crowded around Brenda, and she started to pass out the newspapers. Nancy held out her hand, but Brenda kept skipping over her. Finally

48

Nancy reached out and took one of the papers.

The front page had a headline in big letters. It read, "Dirty Tricks in Class Vote. Funny Faces Are No Joke."

Nancy started to read:

Someone is trying to ruin the class election. And why isn't the person who *says* she's a detective doing anything about it? Is it because her best friends are the ones doing it? Or is *she* a part of it, too?

Bess and George hurried over to Nancy. "I can't believe this," Bess said. "Brenda made it sound like we made all those funny faces."

"I know," Nancy said. "But you know what bothers me more?"

Nancy pointed to a line at the end of the article: "We haven't seen the last of the funny faces. Watch the *Carlton News* for all the details."

"It's as if she knows ahead of time," Nancy said.

50

George stared at her. "Do you really think that Brenda—"

"I don't know," Nancy said. "But I'm going to find out."

During lunch Nancy went over to Brenda's table. Brenda and Lizzie were talking. Brenda was writing in her reporter's notebook. When Brenda and Lizzie saw Nancy, they stopped talking.

"Brenda? Why did you go back to the classroom yesterday?" Nancy asked.

Brenda looked up at her. "Who says I did?"

"I have a witness," Nancy told her. "You were the last to leave the room."

"What if I was?" Brenda replied. "It's none of your business."

"Did you notice a mustache on Bess's poster yesterday?" Nancy asked.

"Maybe I did and maybe I didn't," Brenda said.

Then Lizzie gave Nancy a mean smile.

"So, has the great Nancy Drew

solved the mystery yet?" she asked. "Or are you part of it?"

"What do you mean?" Nancy asked.

"You'll see," Brenda said. She and Lizzie laughed. "You're not the only one who can figure things out."

"Listen, Brenda, was the mustache on Bess's poster there when you left or not?" Nancy asked.

"No comment," Brenda said. "That's newspaper talk. It means, go away and stop bugging me."

Brenda looked down at her notebook again. She and Lizzie acted as if Nancy wasn't there.

After a moment Nancy walked away. Sometimes Brenda made her so mad.

I didn't get any answers from Brenda, Nancy thought. But I know she's up to something.

Then Nancy sat down at a table by herself. She wanted to think about the case. After Nancy ate her lunch, she took out her blue notebook to review her clues. Then she wrote:

Question: Who could have put the mustache on Bess's poster?

Jason
1. Had construction paper
2. In class early this morning
Brenda
1. Last one seen in class yesterday
2. Acts like she's up to something

When she had finished, Nancy walked over to where George and Bess were sitting.

"Howb's duh cathe gobing?" George asked. She was still chewing her peanut butter sandwich.

"IIere, George." Bess giggled. "Have some milk." She passed her milk over to George.

Nancy smiled. "I have a lot of clues. I just haven't figured out what they mean."

Nancy opened her book. She looked at her list of suspects. "And there's something else that's strange."

"What is it?" Bess asked.

"Well," Nancy said. "Lizzie's been really mean to you, right?"

"Yeah," Bess said. "*She* could have put the mustache on my poster."

"But why would Lizzie want to ruin my button?" George asked. "It was for Vicki."

"That's what I don't understand," Nancy said. "But I think Lizzie should be a suspect." Nancy wrote Lizzie's name in her notebook.

When lunch period was over, Mrs. Reynolds's class lined up to go back to their classroom. Nancy, Bess, and George were at the end of the line. Just as they were about to enter the classroom, Nancy heard a horrible scream.

"Noooooo!" the voice cried. It was Vicki!

7

Vicki Blows Up

Nancy, Bess, and George rushed into the classroom. Vicki was staring at the poster she had painted. Someone had drawn another funny face and taped it to her poster.

Vicki grabbed the cartoon and yanked at it. There was a loud tearing sound. Vicki's poster ripped in half.

Vicki stared at the ruined poster. Tears ran down her cheeks. She crumpled up the cartoon and threw it on the floor. Then she turned and pointed her finger at George.

"Brenda and Lizzie warned me," Vicki sobbed. "They said I shouldn't trust you. They were right!"

Nancy glanced around. Brenda was

standing nearby. She had a smile on her face.

"It's just like it said in the newspaper," Vicki declared. She wiped her cheeks. "It's you, Bess, and Nancy. You're all ganging up on me."

"We are not!" Bess cried.

"That's what *you* say!" Lizzie said.

Nancy noticed that Brenda had her red notebook out. She was writing down everything everyone said.

"I don't care what Brenda told you," George said. "She's just trying to make trouble. We didn't do anything to your poster." George stepped closer to Vicki. "Besides, Vicki, I'm on your election team."

"Not anymore," Vicki said. "I don't want you on my team. I don't trust you."

George looked at her. Her mouth was open. "But, Vicki—" she started to say.

"Old friends are the best friends," Vicki said. "Come on, Lizzie. I don't want to be around these snakes."

Vicki and Lizzie walked arm in arm to the other side of the room.

George turned to Nancy and Bess. She looked hurt. "Vicki will be sorry for saying those things when she finds out the truth."

"But first *we* need to find out the truth," Nancy said.

Mrs. Reynolds came into the room. She walked to the front and clapped her hands. "Okay," she called. "Everyone take out your reading books. We're going to read aloud."

Nancy picked up the crumpled cartoon from the floor before she went to her seat. She smoothed it out. The funny face was drawn on plain white paper. The face had ears that stuck out and eyes pointing in two directions. The smile was so goofy that Nancy had to laugh.

"This is pretty funny," she said. "Whoever did this can draw well."

George looked over her shoulder. "You know what?" she said. "I think I've seen something like it before."

"Me, too," Nancy said. "But where? Was it copied from a comic book?"

Nancy folded the cartoon. She took

it to her desk and tucked it into her blue notebook. The notebook was filling up with evidence. But Nancy still couldn't figure out this case.

Nancy thought. The pranks were done to posters for Vicki and Jessie. But who would want to make them *both* look silly?

Jason, of course. He wanted Mike to be president.

Nancy couldn't forget about Brenda, though. The more dirty tricks there were, the more Brenda could write about them.

Lizzie might want to ruin a poster for Jessie but not for Vicki. They were best friends.

What about the latest drawing? Could Jason or Brenda draw like that? Or had it been done by someone Nancy hadn't thought of?

"Nancy," Mrs. Reynolds said. "Would you read the next passage for us?"

Nancy jumped. She had no idea what was going on. And Mrs. Reynolds knew it, too!

Bess leaned close to Nancy. "Top of page thirty-two," she whispered.

Nancy found the place. She started to read.

When the final bell rang, everybody jumped up and started talking at once. Nancy heard Jessie say loudly, "I don't believe it. They wouldn't do something like that."

"That's us they're talking about," Bess whispered to Nancy. She started gathering her books. "Everybody heard what Vicki said before. I think a lot of them believe what she said."

Toward the front of the room, Nancy saw George go over to Vicki. Vicki turned and looked the other way. Then George walked toward Nancy and Bess. She looked upset.

"Some people just won't listen," George said when she reached Nancy and Bess. "Too bad for them."

The three friends walked out into the hall. Some of the kids near the cubbies gave them dirty looks.

"Let's get out of here," George said. She grabbed her jacket from her cubby.

Jenny March let out a gasp. She was staring at George's feet.

Nancy looked down. What was the matter? A bug? A mouse? Then she saw it.

On the floor right in front of George's cubby was a sheet of construction paper—*black* construction paper. A piece was cut out of the middle. The hole was in the shape of a thin squiggly mustache.

8

The Proof

I _knew_ it!" Brenda shouted. "There's the proof. George put that mustache on Bess's poster. I bet you're all in it together."

"Why would _we_ want to ruin Bess's poster, Brenda?" Nancy asked.

"I don't know," Brenda said. "But when I find out, I'm going to write about it in the _Carlton News_. And the whole school will know!"

Brenda stomped away.

Nancy picked up the sheet of black paper. Then she took the mustache from her notebook. It fit perfectly.

"Nancy, I never saw that before," George said. "Somebody must have put it in my cubby."

Bess walked over to George and touched her shoulder. "I know you didn't do it," she said.

Nancy looked around. Some of the kids wouldn't meet her eyes. Did they really think that she, Bess, and George had done this?

"Let's go home," George said. She turned and walked down the hallway to the front door. Nancy and Bess followed her. They were about to leave the school when Jessie caught up to them.

"Listen, guys," Jessie said. "I don't want to run for class president anymore."

"Why not, Jessie?" Nancy asked.

"I thought it would be fun," Jessie said. "But it isn't. Everyone is acting so mean."

"You can't quit now," Bess said.

"But some of the kids are saying that I'm in on all the trouble," Jessie said. "If I'm not running, they won't suspect me."

"Jessie?" Nancy said. "If I find out who did the funny faces, will you still run?"

Jessie hesitated. "Well, I guess so," she said. "But you'll have to figure things out by tomorrow. I have to tell Mrs. Reynolds before everyone votes."

Nancy spent the rest of the afternoon with Bess and George at Bess's house. She didn't have much fun, though. She was too busy thinking about everything that had happened. What if she couldn't solve the mystery? Would Jessie really quit? Would all the kids hate her, Bess, and George?

The next morning Nancy walked to school by herself. All the way there, she was thinking about the mystery.

On the way to her classroom, she walked past the fifth-grade rooms. Something on the bulletin board caught her eye. It was a funny cartoon. The face had crossed eyes, big ears, and a goofy smile.

Nancy stopped and stared at it. Then she took out the one from Vicki's poster. The two faces were practically the same. But the one on the wall had the artist's name on it. Sharon Artello—Lizzie's older sister!

Why would a fifth-grader ruin a third-grader's artwork? Nancy wondered. It didn't make sense. Lizzie must have taken her sister's drawing and used it. But why would Lizzie wreck her best friend's poster? And how could Nancy prove it?

Nancy stared at the funny face drawing in her hand. She noticed something she hadn't noticed before. The tape was still on the top edge. It was clear tape. One part had blue paint on it. The paint was on the sticky side. That must be from Vicki's ruined poster, Nancy thought.

But there was something else. It was below the blue paint. It looked like gold paint, with little specks of red glitter. This was just the proof Nancy was looking for. It was a fingerprint!

Whoever had taped the funny face on Vicki's poster must have had gold paint and red glitter on his or her hands. Some had come off on the sticky tape.

When the bell rang, Nancy rushed

into her classroom. The election posters were hanging on the back wall. The buttons were on Mrs. Reynolds's desk. Nancy looked at the buttons one by one. Only one had gold paint and red glitter on it—Lizzie's. That was the proof Nancy needed.

Lizzie and Vicki came into the classroom. "Get away from my button," Lizzie said. "What are you doing?"

"Finding out the truth," Nancy replied. She held up the cartoon. "Your sister drew this. And you taped it to Vicki's poster."

Lizzie's face reddened. "Who says? Prove it!" she said.

Nancy pointed to the funny face picture. "This tape has a fingerprint. With gold paint and red glitter, Lizzie. Just like your button!"

Vicki turned to her friend. "Lizzie? Is Nancy right? Did you wreck my poster?"

"I didn't mean to," Lizzie said in a tiny voice. "I didn't know it would tear."

"But why, Lizzie?" Vicki asked. "Didn't you want me to win?"

"Yes, but I felt so awful. You were hanging out with George all the time," Lizzie said. "I put the beard and glasses on George's button because I was mad at her."

"But we were all working on the election together," Vicki said.

"But it was like you weren't my best friend anymore," Lizzie said. "I wanted you to get mad at George. I did the other things so you would think that George, Nancy, and Bess were in on it together. So it would be just you and me again."

"That was a rotten thing to do, Lizzie," Vicki said.

"I know," Lizzie said. "I'm sorry."

Bess and George came into the classroom. Nancy explained what had happened. Then she thought a minute and shook her head.

"But this doesn't add up," Nancy said. "If you wanted Vicki to get mad at George, why did you blame Bess for messing up Vicki's speech at the beginning of the campaign?"

"At first, I really did think Bess was trying to ruin our campaign. Then I realized it was just an accident." Lizzie looked at Bess. "I'm sorry, Bess."

"I guess it's okay," Bess said. She looked at George and smiled. "I know what it's like to think you've lost a best friend."

"Yeah," George said. "It makes you feel really bad."

"I want to apologize to George and Nancy, too," Lizzie said. "I'll never do anything like that again."

"I hope not," George said. "Putting that black paper in my cubby was really mean."

"I didn't do that," Lizzie said. "I don't know how it got there. It was in my notebook."

Nancy started to laugh.

"What's so funny, Nancy?" George asked.

"Remember when you thought Lizzie's notebook was Bess's? You put it in your cubby. The paper must have slipped out then."

"Nancy," George said, "you're a genius!"

Lizzie looked shyly at Vicki. "Can we still be friends?"

"I don't know," Vicki said. "I'm still sort of mad."

Lizzie's eyes filled up with tears again. She started to turn away.

"Hey, Lizzie, wait!" Vicki said quickly. "I'm not *that* mad." She gave Lizzie a hug.

Brenda came into the room.

"What's going on?" She rushed over to the group. "What are you guys doing?"

"Oh, nothing, Brenda." Nancy smiled at the others. "We just solved a mystery."

The class election was held that afternoon. Mrs. Reynolds passed out slips of paper to all the students. They were all wearing their buttons.

Nancy wrote "Jessie" on her paper. Then she folded it twice.

Mrs. Reynolds asked Molly to collect the ballots. Then Mrs. Reynolds unfolded them and read each name aloud. Peter stood at the chalkboard and kept count. When they finished, it read:

MIKE MINELLI	IIII III	8
JESSIE SHAPIRO	IIII IIII II	12
VICKI WOLF	IIII	5

"Our new class president is Jessie Shapiro," Mrs. Reynolds announced. "Congratulations, Jessie," she said. "Will you come up here?"

Grinning, Jessie stood up and walked to the front of the room. Everybody clapped.

"Way to go, Jessie," Bess said.

"Thanks, everybody," Jessie said. "And if it's okay, I want Mike and Vicki to be my vice presidents."

Mike and Vicki both waved and nodded.

Jessie's grin widened. "One more thing," she said. "I want to make Nancy Drew our official class detective!"

The whole class cheered.

At home that afternoon, Nancy wrote in her special blue notebook.

I finally solved the case of the Funny Face Fight. I learned something about friendship, too. You can make new friends without giving up your old friends. New or old, good friends are the best!
Case closed.

TAKE A RIDE
WITH THE KIDS ON BUS FIVE!

Natalie Adams and James Penny have just started
third grade. They like their teacher, and they like
Maple Street School. The only trouble is, they have
to ride bad old Bus Five to get there!

#1 THE BAD NEWS BULLY
Can Natalie and James stop the bully on Bus Five?

#2 WILD MAN AT THE WHEEL
When Mr. Balter calls in sick,
the kids get some strange new drivers.

#3 FINDERS KEEPERS
The kids on Bus Five keep losing things.
Is there a thief on board?
Coming mid-September '96

#4 I SURVIVED ON BUS FIVE
Bad luck turns into big fun
when Bus Five breaks down in a rainstorm.
Coming mid-October '96

BY MARCIA LEONARD
ILLUSTRATED BY JULIE DURRELL

 A MINSTREL® BOOK

Published by Pocket Books

1237-01